¡Hola! I'm Dora and this is Boots. Today I have really exciting news. Someone new is going to join my family! It's someone who sleeps in a cradle, drinks from a bottle, wears diapers, and likes to be rocked to sleep! Can you guess who it is?

A baby! *¡Sí!* My *mami* is going to have a baby! Boots says I'm going to be a great big sister. And he's going to teach the baby to do the Monkey Dance! Let's hurry home—the baby is coming right now! We need to find the quickest way to my house.

Map says first we have to go through the Spooky Forest. Then we have to go through the Nut Farm. And that's how we'll get to my house. Hurry! My *mami's* having a baby!

Look! It's the Spooky Forest. And there's Isa the iguana.
Isa! Isa! My *mami's* having a baby! I'm going to be a great
big sister, Boots will teach the baby the Monkey Dance, . . . and
you can teach the baby about flowers, plants, and butterflies.

There are lots of spooky animals in the Spooky Forest, like snakes and crocodiles.

We need to take the path with the Friendly Frog. Should we take the first path, the second path, or the third path?

The third path! Right! Smart looking! We made it through the Spooky Forest. Next we need to go to the Nut Farm. Do you see the Nut Farm? I see it too! And there's our friend Benny the bull.

Benny! Benny! My *mami's* having a baby! I'm going to be a great big sister, Boots will teach the baby the Monkey Dance, Isa can teach the baby about flowers, plants, and butterflies, . . . and you can give the baby piggyback rides.

The Nut Farm is far away, but Benny says he will drive us if we can help him put the tires on his go-cart. Let's count the tires in Spanish. *Uno, dos, tres, cuatro.*

We made it to the Nut Farm! And there's our friend Tico with his cousins!

Tico! Tico! *¡Mi mami va a tener un bebé!* My *mami's* having a baby!

Tico says he can teach the baby how to speak Spanish. *Gracias,* Tico!

Map says we need to go to my house next. Do you see my house? There it is! Come on! We have to get home quickly. My *mami's* having a baby!

Look! My whole family is here! They are wearing *capias*, special pins to celebrate the baby. My *papi* says the baby is here too—that means I'm a big sister!

My *papi* also says he has an even bigger surprise. What can it be?

Twins! My *mami* had two babies. I have a baby brother *and* a baby sister.

¡Hola! I'm your big sister, Dora. Someday you'll go exploring with me!

Look! The babies smiled at me!

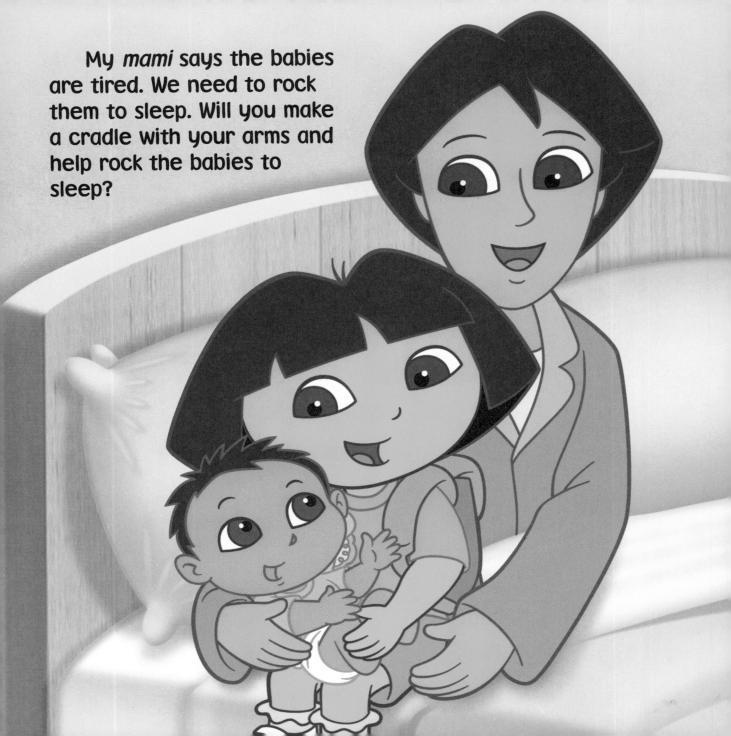

My *mami* says the babies are tired. We need to rock them to sleep. Will you make a cradle with your arms and help rock the babies to sleep?

Great rocking! The babies are asleep.

We did it! *¡Lo hicimos!* Thanks for helping me get home quickly to see my new baby brother and sister!